Day by Day

Susan Gal

Alfred A. Knopf

Heart to heart, for Jim

THIS IS A BORZOI BOOK
PUBLISHED BY ALFRED A. KNOPF

Visit us on the Web! randomhouse.com/kids
Educators and librarians, for a variety of teaching tools, visit us at
randomhouse.com/teachers

Library of Congress Cataloging-in-Publication Data is
available upon request.
ISBN: 978-0-375-86959-4 (trade)
ISBN: 978-0-375-96959-1 (lib. bdg.)

MANUFACTURED IN CHINA
July 2012
10 9 8 7 6 5 4 3 2 1
First Edition

Mile by mile, pigs motor west.

Brick by brick, pigs build a house . . .

and piece by piece, it becomes a home.

Neighbor by neighbor, pigs say, "Welcome!"

Arm in arm, new friendships begin.

Then row by row, pigs plant a garden.

And inch by inch, the garden grows.

Day by day, the seasons turn.

Shoulder to shoulder, pigs gather the harvest.

Layer by layer, pigs shed their clothes . . .

and one by one, pigs cannonball!

Hand in hand, pigs give thanks.

Then cheek to cheek, they dance.

Yawn by yawn, pigs head for home.

Kiss by kiss, pigs say good night . . .

and dream sweet dreams night after night.